The Kiss of Calamity

by: Debbie Joyce

Illustrated by: Nina Flores

ISBN 978-1-0879-7237-4

To my Dad,
Who always makes me laugh!
Debbie

Let me tell you a story,
When I was just a kid.
You may not believe it happened,
But I promise that it did!

I blew my mom a kiss one day, and it knocked her to the floor.

Then the very kiss I blew, went flying out the door!

It flew right past a cowboy, which brought him to his knees.

And as it passed some songbirds,
They fell out of the trees!

Some neighbor kids were playing ball,
When it knocked them to the ground.

I said, "This kiss is crazy! This kiss, it must be found!"

I put my boots and hat on,
And I reached for my lasso.
If I was going to catch my kiss,
I had to do it pronto!

As I walked through the fields,
I saw that damage had been done.

Not a rancher was left standing—cows were gagging by the ton!

I searched all around, to the left and to the right.

I looked up high and down below,
While the day turned into night.

Walking along I shook my head,
And then I spotted the kiss.

I swung my lasso round and round, and made sure I didn't miss!

The kiss, it was a wild thing, pulling at my lasso.

But I held on tight
And brought it close.
And Boy!
What do ya know!

I wondered why a simple kiss
Had made everyone so sick!
But one big whiff made me recall,
That my lunch was filled with garlic!

What in the world had I eaten for lunch?
It was some spicy chili,
Made by the best cook in town,
My dear sweet, old Aunt Millie.

All the ranchers, kids and cows, were very proud of me!

Old Town
TOYS & GAMES
CONVENIENCE STORE
OPEN
7am-7pm
Mon-Sat
HAR

Aunt Millie was so thrilled,
That my stinky kiss was caught.
So, she took me to the store,
And for me, mint gum she bought.

The town recovered quickly,
From that awfully smelly kiss.
But I don't eat chili anymore,
And that's something I really miss.

What, you say you don't believe me?
You think I've told a lie?
Here's a bowl of chili —
I dare you to give it a try.

Then blow your mom a kiss, and watch it fly around,
Causing ruin and calamity, as it blows throughout your town!

CPSIA information can be obtained
at www.ICGtesting.com
Printed in the USA
BVRC090903230921
617361BV00001BA/7